The LAST FIREHAWK

The Golden Temple

by
Katrina Charman

BRANCHES™

SCHOLASTIC INC.

The LAST FIREHAWK

Read All the Books

scholastic.com/lastfirehawk

Table of Contents

For Maddie, Piper, and Riley. –KC
For Lili and Zaza. –JT

Text copyright © 2020 by Katrina Charman
Illustrations by Judit Tondora copyright © 2020 by Scholastic Inc.

Library of Congress Cataloging-in-Publication Data

Names: Charman, Katrina, author. | Tondora, Judit, illustrator. | Charman, Katrina. Last firehawk ; 9.
Title: The golden temple / by Katrina Charman ; [illustrated by Judit Tondora].
Description: First edition. | New York, NY : Branches/Scholastic Inc., 2020. | Series: The last firehawk ; 9 | Summary: Tag, Skyla, and Blaze are on a new quest to find Blaze's family, and Thorn's twin brother, Claw (who claims to be nothing like his evil brother), has offered to guide them to the mysterious Golden Temple where the firehawks were last seen; but the jungle is full of dangers and Tag is not sure they can trust Claw--and even if they find the firehawks, will that help them return to their home in Perodia?
Identifiers: LCCN 2019059410 (print) | LCCN 2019059411 (ebook) | ISBN 9781338565348 (paperback) | ISBN 9781338565355 (library binding) | ISBN 9781338565362 (ebook)
Subjects: LCSH: Owls—Juvenile fiction. | Squirrels—Juvenile fiction. | Animals, Mythical—Juvenile fiction. | Magic—Juvenile fiction. | Quests (Expeditions)—Juvenile fiction. | Adventure stories. | CYAC: Owls—Fiction. | Squirrels—Fiction. | Animals, Mythical—Fiction. | Magic—Fiction. | Adventure and adventurers—Fiction. | Fantasy. | LCGFT: Action and adventure fiction.
Classification: LCC PZ7.1.C495 Go 2020 (print) | LCC PZ7.1.C495 (ebook) | DDC [Fic]—dc23
LC record available at https://lccn.loc.gov/2019059410
LC ebook record available at https://lccn.loc.gov/2019059411

10 9 8 7 6 5 4 3 2   20 21 22 23 24

Printed in China   62

First edition, October 2020
Illustrated by Judit Tondora
Edited by Rachel Matson
Book design by Maria Mercado

~ INTRODUCTION ~

Tag, a small barn owl, and his friends Skyla, a squirrel, and Blaze, a firehawk, are in the magical land of the Cloud Kingdom. When they were in the land of Perodia, Tag, Skyla, and Blaze defeated the evil vulture, Thorn. They stopped Thorn from destroying Perodia and stealing the magical Ember Stone. Now they are searching for clues to find Blaze's family: the lost firehawks. There are many strange sights to see in the Cloud Kingdom, and new creatures to meet.

The most mysterious creature of all is the vulture Claw. He says he is Thorn's twin brother and that he is good, unlike his evil brother. Tag isn't sure he can trust Claw, but Tag, Skyla, and Blaze must learn to trust him. Claw has promised to lead them to the Golden Temple, the place where the firehawks were last seen and where Blaze might finally find her family.

The adventure continues . . .

THE CLOUD

Golden Temple

Snappers Stream

Twisty Trees

Crystal Pass

N
W · E
S

THE LONG JOURNEY

Tag, Skyla, and Blaze sat on a rock in a patch of grass. They ate the last of their fruit and nuts. Claw stood in front of them, walking back and forth.

"We need to get moving," Claw said. "We have a long way to go before we reach the Golden Temple."

"How far away is it?" Blaze asked.

"A few hours, at least," Claw replied. "The temple is hidden within a thick jungle. It is very hard to find."

Tag turned his back to peek inside his sack. The Ember Stone and the golden feathers were still safe inside.

He turned back to Claw. "Are you sure you know the way?" Tag asked.

"Yes," Claw said. "But it has been a long time since I last saw the firehawks. If they do not want to be found, it may be impossible to find them. Unless—"

"Unless what?" Skyla asked, tucking her slingshot into her armor.

"Unless you have any clues?" Claw said slowly, looking at Tag's sack.

Tag shook his head quickly. "Our only clue is what you've told us about the Golden Temple. That's why we need your help, Claw."

Claw nodded. "Well, if you've finished eating, we should continue on," he said.

He walked off into the trees.

"Shouldn't we fly?" Blaze called out, hurrying to catch up.

"It is better if we go on foot," Claw replied. "The jungle is very overgrown. We won't be able to spot the Golden Temple from the sky."

They walked on through the Cloud Kingdom. In the distance, Tag saw the Rainbow Waterfall, where Blaze had been taken by the giant birds.

The friends soon reached a wide stream. It sparkled different shades of blue.

"Oh no!" Tag said, remembering they had been here before. "Watch out for the snappy fish!"

Then a large fish leaped from the water!
It snapped its sharp teeth at Blaze.

"Aghhhh!" Blaze yelled, stepping back.

"This is Snappers Stream," Claw told
them. "Be careful. Those fish bite!"

"I remember," said Skyla, gripping her tail
tightly.

She jumped onto Blaze's back.

The friends flew over the hungry fish in Snappers Stream and landed on the other side.

"Phew," Tag said. "I'm glad we flew across this time."

Suddenly, a loud hum filled the air. In the sky, heading right for them, was a cloud of angry-looking bugs.

STORM BUGS!

"**S**torm bugs!" Claw cried. "We must leave, now!"

Skyla jumped onto Blaze's back, and the friends flew away from the bugs. Tag glanced behind him. The bugs were as big as he was, with large, round bubble-bottoms that sparked with flashes of lightning.

"They are following us!" Blaze cried.

"Fly faster," Claw shouted. "We don't want them to catch up to us."

"What will happen if they *do*?" Skyla asked.

A flash of lightning hit a tree behind them. The tree exploded into flames.

"*That's* what!" Claw said.

Tag gulped. He flew faster, as lightning flashed and raindrops began falling on his feathers. A deafening crack of thunder echoed around them.

Why are these bugs chasing us? he wondered. The storm bugs seemed very angry at them.

The friends flew over the thick jungle. All Tag could see below were the green treetops, which spread in all directions. As he flew, his wings felt more and more tired.

"The storm bugs aren't slowing down!" Tag called. "We need to hide."

He pointed to the trees below.

Blaze led the way, swooping l[...] she disappeared into the trees. Cla[w] followed.

"Hurry," Claw said, racing into the jungle. The storm bugs buzzed above the treetops. They sounded close.

Tag tried to keep up with the others, but Skyla was leaping from branch to branch. Blaze and Claw were moving just as fast.

"Wait up!" Tag puffed. But his friends were too far away to hear!

BZZZZZZZZZZZZZ!

Tag tripped over a twisty vine. His foot was caught! He pulled and pulled, but it wouldn't come free.

The buzzing came closer. Flashes of lightning moved through the trees until the storm bugs were hovering right above him. They formed an enormous dark cloud.

Tag grabbed his dagger and cut at the vine, trying to get free. But he was stuck.

Then suddenly—

SKRAAAAAAAAA!

Blaze soared through the trees, letting out her powerful firehawk cry.

The storm bugs flew around in circles, bumping into one another. Skyla and Claw ran to Tag.

The storm bugs stopped and glared at Claw. One of the bugs began flying around so quickly that it was a yellow blur.

"I think that bug is writing a message in the air," Tag said.

Skyla narrowed her eyes. "What does it say?" she asked.

The storm bug finished writing.

Blaze slowly read the word. *"BEWARE!"*

BEWARE!

The storm bugs turned and buzzed away. Tag watched them leave, his eyes wide.

"Are you okay?" Skyla asked Tag.

Tag finally pulled his foot free from the vine and nodded. "I don't think the bugs were trying to hurt us," he said. "I think they wanted to warn us."

"About what?" Blaze asked.

Tag looked at Claw. He was sure that the storm bugs had looked right at the old vulture when they'd spelled out the message: *Beware!*

What were they trying to tell us? he wondered.

"Maybe they were warning us about the jungle?" Claw suggested. "We're lucky we have a firehawk to protect us."

Blaze smiled.

The friends made their way through the jungle. The trees were tall and thick with long, curvy leaves that touched the ground. Twisty green vines wound around the trunks and along the ground. As they walked, the air grew hot.

Tag could hear the sound of hundreds of insects chirping and humming to one another. He held his dagger tight as he looked around for any other dangerous creatures.

"How far is the temple from here?" Blaze asked Claw.

Claw looked unsure. "It has been a long time since I was there. The jungle has grown even thicker."

"Maybe the map can help us?" Skyla whispered to Tag.

Tag moved away from Claw and unrolled the map. It showed a picture of green trees. In the center was a small picture of Tag, Blaze, Skyla, and Claw.

There was no sign of the Golden Temple.

"I think we're lost," Tag said.

Blaze frowned. "Well, let's keep following this path."

Tag cut at the thick vines hanging in their way. The farther they walked, the smaller the path became.

Soon, there was no path at all. They were surrounded by trees and bushes on all sides.

"Are you sure you know where you are going, Claw?" Tag grumbled.

Claw ignored him. "Use your firepower to make a path, Blaze," he said.

"No!" Blaze cried. "My firepower could burn down the jungle. We'll have to clear the path without using my powers."

Together, the friends pulled at the vines and bushes. Tag used his dagger to cut a way through.

"Skyla," Tag whispered. "I think Claw is lost."

Skyla frowned. "Try checking the map again," she whispered.

Tag reached into his sack when Blaze suddenly shouted.

"The temple!" Blaze cried, jumping up and down. "We've found the Golden Temple!"

THE DISCOVERY

The friends raced forward. The temple stood in the middle of a large clearing surrounded by palm trees. The temple's stone walls were old and crumbling, and most of the roof had fallen down. The walls were covered in moss and vines.

"It doesn't look like the firehawks have
been here for a long time," Skyla said.

Tag nodded. "Are you sure this is where you last saw the firehawks?" he asked Claw.

"It was long ago," Claw said. "But yes, I am sure."

Blaze hopped closer. "This temple is in ruins," she said sadly. "Even if my family was here at some point, they've been gone for a long time."

Tag patted Blaze on the shoulder, then turned to Claw. "What now?" he asked.

"The firehawks might have left some clues behind," Claw suggested.

"Let's split up and take a look around," said Skyla.

Blaze and Skyla went inside while Claw searched outside.

Tag walked around the other side of the temple, away from Claw. His tummy twisted as he remembered the storm bugs' warning. He looked for anything that might tell them where the firehawks were.

But then, he heard a scream.

"Help!"

It was Skyla!

Tag raced into the temple with Claw following closely behind. He searched for Skyla, but the temple was full of fallen stones.

25

The floor and walls were covered in more vines. Tag cut through them as he made his way through an open doorway.

"Over here!" Skyla shouted. "I'm stuck!"

Tag flew over to Skyla. She was wrapped in something silvery. She wriggled and squirmed, trying to break free.

"What is it?" Tag asked.

"That's a web," Claw said. "A *giant* web."

Tag's feathers trembled. Claw was right. Skyla was caught in a huge *spider's* web. The silvery threads were almost as thick as the vines.

"Help me get out," Skyla cried, "before the spider comes back!"

Tag tried to use his dagger to cut away at the thick, silvery threads.

"The web is too strong. My dagger can't cut through it," Tag puffed.

"Let me try," Claw said. He used his sharp talons and beak to try to break the web. But that didn't work either.

Next, Blaze lit up her feathers and tried to burn through the thread. But no matter what they did, the web would not break.

"Um . . . Tag," Skyla said, her voice trembling. "Something's coming."

Tag froze as a huge hairy leg slowly lowered down into the temple right in front of them. They all looked up. Hanging above them from the cracked ceiling, with its sharp jaws open wide, was the biggest spider Tag had ever seen.

THE WEB

The spider dangled above them. It was twice as tall as Blaze and had a huge, round body. Tag held out his dagger with a shaky wing. Claw grabbed a rock in his talon, and Blaze's feathers lit up.

"Please don't hurt us!" Skyla cried.

The spider watched the friends for a moment with her beady eyes. Then she giggled.

"I won't hurt you," she said. "I heard your cries and came to help!"

Tag frowned. "You don't want to eat us?" he asked.

The spider laughed. "Why would I want to eat you? You are covered in fur and feathers!"

Tag sagged with relief.

"Then could you please let our friend down?" Blaze asked.

The spider crawled onto her web. Skyla squeezed her eyes shut as the spider snipped the threads with her sharp teeth.

Finally, Skyla was free.

"Thank you!" Skyla said, brushing pieces of web from her fur.

"You're welcome." The spider smiled. "I'm Winnie."

"I'm Skyla. These are my friends Tag, Blaze, and Claw," Skyla replied.

"Have you lived in the jungle long?" Blaze asked.

Winnie dropped to the ground. "All my life," she said.

"Have you ever seen any firehawks here?" Blaze asked hopefully. "They look like me."

Winnie thought for a moment. "Sorry," she said. "We don't get many visitors."

"We?" Claw asked.

"My mother and me," the spider said. "And all my brothers and sisters." She pointed to the trees above, which were covered in webs. The vines hung over into the temple through the broken roof.

Tag gulped, hoping that the other spiders wouldn't show up too soon.

"There *is* something you might want to see," Winnie said.

They followed Winnie and found themselves in a large, open hall.

"Look at the floor," Winnie said.

There were four flat stones in the middle of the room. Each one had strange markings scratched into it.

Skyla brushed away dust and dirt with her tail. "Look!" she gasped.

Blaze hopped closer. "Those are feathers," she said.

Each stone held a picture of a long golden feather.

"Is that what you were looking for?" Winnie asked.

"Maybe," Blaze said. "We could be looking for a portal. It is a magical door to another place."

"How do you open a portal?" Winnie asked.

"We'd need a magical object," Claw said.

Tag glanced at Blaze and nodded.

"We have golden feathers," Blaze said. "Show him, Tag."

Tag took out the three golden feathers. Claw's eyes grew wide.

"Those are definitely magical! Do you know what this means?" Claw said. "We can open the portal and find the firehawks!"

"Peep!" Blaze cried, hopping up and down.

"Put the feathers on the stones," Claw said.

Tag placed a golden feather on three of the four flat stones. The friends stepped back.

Tag waited for a portal to appear . . .

FOUR FEATHERS

The temple was still and silent.

"It didn't work," Tag said. His head drooped.

"There are four stones with pictures on them," Claw said. "We must need a fourth feather to open the portal."

"But we only have three," Blaze said.

"Maybe there is one hidden here?" Skyla suggested. "Like the one we found in the Howling Caves."

"I know every nook and cranny of this temple," Winnie said sadly. "If there was a golden feather here, I would have seen it."

Tag sighed. "What now?" he asked.

"I'm sorry," Winnie said. "I wish I could help you. But I have to go. My mom is calling me."

Skyla sank to the floor.

"We can't give up!" Blaze cried.

"We don't have enough feathers to open the portal," Tag said. "We're going to be stuck in the Cloud Kingdom forever."

Blaze's eyes filled with tears. "I will never find my family."

Skyla gave her friend a hug.

Claw looked to Tag. "If only we had *another* magical object," Claw said, raising an eyebrow. "We could try to place that on the fourth stone instead of a golden feather."

Blaze glanced at Tag. Tag's tummy twisted. *Can we trust Claw enough to tell him about the Ember Stone?* he wondered.

"Grey did say that *any* magical object could open a portal," Skyla said.

Tag sighed and opened up his sack. *There's no other way*, he thought.

"We have this," he said, holding out the Ember Stone. It felt cold and heavy in his wing.

Claw gasped. He reached out a wing to touch it, but the Ember Stone flared red hot!

Tag dropped it to the ground.

"Ouch!" Claw cried.

The Ember Stone had been too hot for Thorn to touch, too, Tag remembered.

"Heat can't hurt me," Blaze said. She picked up the stone with her beak and placed it on the fourth flat stone.

Suddenly, the ground beneath them began to shake. Tag held on to Skyla's paw and Blaze's wing. All around them, the stone walls began to crumble.

The three golden feathers lit up, and the Ember Stone glowed purple. A bright swirling light appeared in the temple floor.

"The portal!" Claw shouted. He jumped and disappeared into the light.

"I hope this portal takes us to the firehawks," Tag shouted. He looked at his friends. "Ready?"

Skyla and Blaze nodded. Then they took a deep breath, and jumped!

CHAPTER

7

THE LOST
FIREHAWKS

The world around Tag swirled with color.
Tag felt dizzy. He saw the temple spinning
around them. The Ember Stone and the
golden feathers whizzed by in a rush of colors.
He reached out and grabbed the Ember
Stone.

Finally, he landed with a THUD!

"Tag!" Skyla called, running over to her friend.

"This place is amazing!" Blaze called out, jumping up and down.

Tag looked around. The crumbling temple was gone. In its place was a new temple, but this one wasn't in ruins. It seemed to rise all the way to the sky, with tall towers and shiny pillars. It glittered and shone as brightly as the sun in the blue sky above.

Tag laughed. "Wow! I don't think we're in the Cloud Kingdom anymore!"

Skyla ran toward the temple. "Let's go inside," she suggested. "Maybe the firehawks are here!"

They raced after her, up the steep stone steps. The temple had two tall, golden doors and a statue of a large, golden egg on each side.

"Those are *golden* eggs!" Blaze said. "Just like the golden egg I hatched from! This temple *must* belong to the firehawks!"

Tag knocked on the door, but there was no answer. He pushed it open. "Is anyone here?" he called through the doorway.

Again, there was no answer.
"Let's go in!" Skyla said.

They stepped inside, and Tag stared around in wonder. It was the most beautiful place he had ever seen! There were tall pillars covered in glitter that swirled around in spirals. Curving stairs were carved into the walls and went up, up, up as far as Tag could see. A golden fountain stood in the middle of the long hallway. Sparkling water sprinkled out of it like raindrops. But the water didn't trickle down, it trickled *up*!

"Is this a dream?" Blaze said, rubbing her eyes.

"It must be," Skyla said. "This is all too amazing to be real!"

But Tag didn't see firehawks, or any other creatures either. He paused.

"Where is Claw?" he asked.

"That's strange. He came through the portal right before us," Skyla said. "Maybe he landed somewhere else?"

They entered a smaller room. It was filled with colorful lights that whizzed around making beautiful shapes and patterns.

The friends stared up at the lights in wonder.

"We should look for Claw," Blaze said after a while.

They continued on, down hallways and beneath golden arches.

Finally, they reached an open courtyard. In its center was an egg-shaped pool filled with sparkling blue water. There were tropical flowers and swaying palm trees all around.

A group of birds stood on the other side of the courtyard. They had red and yellow and orange feathers. The birds turned to look at Blaze.

Tag gasped. "The lost firehawks!" he cried. "We found them!"

FAMILY

The firehawks walked to Blaze, whispering to one another. Tag couldn't believe his eyes. There were so many of them! Some tall, some small, some old, and some young.

Tag looked at Skyla, and they grinned at each other. Blaze had the biggest smile they had ever seen! Seeing her this way made his heart happy.

Blaze stepped forward. "My name is Blaze," she told the firehawks. "I was born in Valor Wood, in Perodia. I am looking for my family."

TOOT-TOOOOOOT!

A loud horn echoed around them, and the firehawks moved aside. A tall firehawk with long, elegant feathers appeared and walked through the crowd. She wore a sparkly, jeweled headdress.

Tag whispered to Skyla, "Do you think she's their leader?"

"She must be," Skyla whispered back.

The tall firehawk stopped in front of Blaze. Her eyes narrowed as she looked Blaze up and down. "Is it really you?" the firehawk asked.

Blaze gave a small peep, and the firehawk smiled. She hugged Blaze tightly. "I am Talia. Leader of the firehawks, and your mother. I've missed you so much."

Blaze and Talia wrapped their wings around each other. Talia wiped away tears.

Skyla sniffed, trying not to cry, too.

"I knew that you would find your way back to me," Talia said. "Did you find the clues I left behind?"

Blaze nodded. "We found the paintings on Fire Island and your three golden feathers. My friends Tag and Skyla helped me, too."

Talia smiled at Tag and Skyla. "I am so glad to meet you both," she said. "Welcome to the Land of the Firehawks. Thank you for helping Blaze on this journey."

"Why did you all leave Perodia?" Skyla asked.

"When Thorn became a danger to Valor Wood, Grey, the leader of the Owls of Valor, asked us for help. He told us to hide out on Fire Island, but Thorn and his Shadow became too strong, and he was close to finding us. You see, Thorn wanted our powers for himself. So we had to leave the Land of Perodia and come home. This is a hidden world that only firehawks can find. Without Blaze, you would have been unable to enter the portal."

"You left me behind," Blaze said to her mother. Blaze's feathers drooped.

Talia hugged her daughter. "I had a vision long before you hatched. It showed me that you would save Perodia," she told Blaze. "I had to leave you behind so that you would win the fight against Thorn."

She looked at Tag and Skyla. "I left her egg in the Howling Caves of Valor Wood, hoping that Grey could keep her safe."

Tag glanced at Skyla. *It was lucky we found Blaze's egg*, he thought. *Even Grey hadn't known the egg was there.*

Talia faced them. "It is because of you two that Blaze was able to defeat Thorn and The Shadow," she said.

"You know about that?" Tag asked, amazed.

Talia smiled. "Firehawk leaders have visions of what has been and what will come. I always knew that Blaze would find her way back to me."

Suddenly, Claw stepped forward from behind a pillar.

"You!" Talia cried. She pointed a fiery wing at Claw. "Firehawks, attack!"

The firehawks surrounded Claw. Their feathers burst into flames as they closed in around him. Then Talia threw two fireballs at Claw!

CHAPTER 9

THE ENEMY

Blaze stepped in front of Claw and held out her wings.

"Wait!" she cried.

"Blaze, be careful!" Talia said. She turned to Claw. "How did you get here, Thorn?"

"He's not Thorn," Tag said quickly. He didn't want to see Claw turned into toast. "He's Thorn's twin brother, Claw."

Talia narrowed her eyes at the vulture. "I didn't know Thorn had a brother," she said.

"Claw is our friend," Skyla said. "He saved my life in the Cloud Kingdom."

Claw nodded quickly. "I'm not here to hurt anyone," he said. "I just want to go home. I need your help getting back to Perodia."

Talia waved a wing at the other firehawks, and their flames went out. "Is this true, Blaze?" she asked.

"Yes," Blaze said. "Claw helped us find the Golden Temple. We would never have found you without his help."

Talia watched Claw carefully. "Thorn would *never* have helped my daughter," she said.

"I am not like my brother," Claw said.

Talia nodded. "If Blaze trusts you, then so do I," she said. She looked at Tag, Skyla, and Blaze and smiled. "Let me show you all around."

"I actually need to rest," Claw said. "This has all been very tiring."

A firehawk showed Claw where he could sleep, while Tag and the others followed Talia outside.

The temple was on a small island surrounded by a golden sandy beach and clear blue water. Along the beach were small wooden huts where the firehawks lived.

Talia introduced them to some of the other firehawks.

"This is Maya," Talia said. "She is our healer. She helps anyone who is ill or hurt."

"Welcome home," the older firehawk said to Blaze. Tag could see her hut had rows of small bottles filled with colorful liquids.

They moved on to the next hut. "And this is Melody," Talia said. "She has the most wonderful singing voice you've ever heard."

Melody sang, and Tag couldn't help but hum along. The song was beautiful. Blaze swayed back and forth with the music. When the song was over, they said goodbye to Melody and walked on.

"What's that up ahead?" Blaze asked, pointing to a big pile of branches and sticks.

Talia smiled. "It's a nest," she said. She moved a few palm leaves aside. Six golden eggs rested inside.

"These eggs are almost ready to hatch," Talia told them. "There is a special ceremony that takes place when the nest catches fire. The baby firehawks rise from the ashes."

Tag remembered how the old oak tree had caught fire when Blaze hatched. He had found her in the ashes.

"I'm sorry I wasn't there to see you hatch," Talia told Blaze.

"Maybe I could take part in the ceremony when these eggs hatch?" Blaze suggested.

"That is a wonderful idea, Blaze! Your friends can help, too," Talia said.

"Even Claw?" Blaze asked.

Talia smiled. "Yes, even Claw."

Tag's tummy churned. *I should feel excited for Blaze*, he thought, *so why do I feel so worried?*

TALIA'S GIFT

For several days, Tag, Blaze, Skyla, and Claw spent time with the firehawks and explored the island.

One day, Tag and Skyla were playing on the beach. Talia was teaching Blaze more about her powers.

"Look, Tag!" Blaze called out. Tag watched as his friend opened her beak wide. But instead of her loud cry, she gave a softer **SKRAAAAAA**. A coconut shell that was nearby began to float in the air.

"That is so cool!" Skyla said.

"That's not *all* I've learned." Blaze smiled. "Check this out."

Her feathers lit up one by one with small flames. She pointed at the sky, then waved her wings in the air. Hundreds of tiny colorful fireballs shot out. They exploded, and little sparkles rained down like fireworks.

"Pretty!" Skyla said, clapping.

"It's also a good way to call for help," Talia told them.

Blaze grinned at Talia. "Show them the gifts," Blaze said.

Talia pulled something from her feathers and handed it to Skyla. "This is for you," she said. "To thank you for bringing Blaze home."

Skyla looked at the gift. It was a golden slingshot.

"Wow!" Skyla said. "Thank you!"

"Try it out," Tag said.

Skyla grinned and picked up a small pebble on the beach. She put it into her slingshot and shot it out to sea. The pebble flew far, until it was out of sight.

"Whoa!" Skyla said. "I'm going to need more pebbles!"

"Is the slingshot magic?" Tag asked.

"This land is magical. Everything made here has some kind of special power," Talia said.

"Show Tag *his* gift," Blaze said.

Talia smiled. "I have something special for you, too, Tag," Talia said.

She handed Tag a small glass bottle. It was filled with a swirly, bright green liquid.

"What does it do?" Tag asked.

"Drink one drop," Talia said.

Tag opened the bottle and let a drop drip into his beak. Suddenly, his wings started flapping. They moved faster and faster until they were a blur.

"Fly!" Talia told him.

He flew faster than he had ever flown before. He zoomed through the trees, in and out, and over the wooden huts along the beach.

"This liquid gives me special flying powers! It is amazing!" Tag whooped. He flew until his wings started to slow down.

Then he landed beside his friends.

"The magic doesn't last long," Talia said. "But it can help if you are ever in danger or need to get somewhere fast."

"Thank you," Tag said, putting the bottle into his sack.

"There is one more surprise," Talia said.

They followed her down the beach where the firehawks had gathered. A big feast was laid out on a table. Music was playing, and the firehawks were dancing. A big banner hanging over the table read: WELCOME HOME, BLAZE!

Blaze and Skyla hurried down to the party. Claw was standing a little way away, watching the firehawks.

Tag looked to Claw. The vulture seemed a bit lost, and Tag felt sorry for him.

"Come on," Tag said. "Let's join in."

Claw paused for a moment, then he smiled and followed Tag down to the beach. The friends and the firehawks laughed and danced all night under the bright moon.

Later, as Tag settled down to sleep, he thought about the fact that Blaze was home now.

I'm happy she's home, Tag thought, *but what happens when we return to Perodia? Will we have to leave Blaze behind?*

CHAPTER 11

HATCHING DAY

The Land of the Firehawks was very busy the morning of the ceremony. Skyla weaved garlands from vines and flowers to hang as decorations. Tag gathered fruit and nuts. Even Claw was helping out by keeping a close eye on the golden eggs.

Everyone was very excited about the
ceremony, especially Blaze.

"I can't wait to see the firehawks hatch!" she said. Blaze flew from one side of the temple's great hall to the other to hang up Skyla's decorations.

Blaze landed next to her friends. "It was amazing when you hatched," Tag told her.

"At least we know what to expect this time," Skyla said. "When *your* egg caught fire, we thought something terrible had happened!"

Tag placed the food he had gathered into large golden bowls. He laid them out on the long table.

"The hall looks wonderful," Talia said, looking around. "It is time to begin."

TOOT-TOOOOT!

A loud trumpet sounded. Soon the hall was filled with hundreds of firehawks waiting for the ceremony to start.

"The hatching ceremony helps new firehawks gain control over their powers right away," Talia said. "All firehawks are born into fire. It gives us strength and power. It shows us the way to the light—the way to know what is good."

Blaze nodded.

There was another loud trumpeting sound.

TOOT-TOOOOT!

Two firehawks started banging on drums. They led the way through the crowd, with Talia following behind. Tag, Blaze, Skyla, and Claw walked beside the leader of the firehawks.

The rest of the firehawks followed in a line.

Once everyone was outside the temple, they gathered around the nest. The six golden eggs looked shinier than ever. Tag thought they might even be glowing.

"Blaze," Talia called. "Step into the nest."

Tag patted Blaze's shoulder. "Good luck!" he said.

Blaze smiled and climbed into the nest.

The drums stopped, and everyone was silent.

Then, one by one, the eggs lit up. They burst into golden flames, which reached higher and higher until Tag couldn't see Blaze anymore.

The fire died down, and the eggs cracked open.

"It's beautiful!" Claw said, watching the firehawks hatch.

A baby firehawk popped out of each egg.

Blaze's feathers lit up.

Suddenly—

BOOM! There was a huge explosion. Tag pulled Skyla down to the ground, covering her with his wing.

He glanced up to see what had happened. There, in the middle of the nest, was a giant ball of silver fire, glowing like the Ember Stone. But it wasn't the Ember Stone.

It was Blaze!

CHAPTER 12

BLAZE'S POWERS

T ag stepped toward Blaze. His eyes were wide as he watched the silver flames swirl around her.

"She will be fine," Talia told him.

Skyla held on to Tag's wing. "Is the fire supposed to be silver?" she asked.

"The hatching ceremony gives a firehawk their special powers. Blaze didn't have a hatching ceremony, so she had to wait for her powers to grow," Talia explained. "I think that is why the flames are silver. Now, she will be even more powerful."

The firehawks began chanting a low song. It got louder and louder, and Melody sang loudest of all. Then the firehawks held up their wings to the sky, and out shot hundreds of small fireballs.

"Wow!" Tag cried. It was beautiful.

The fireballs floated away on the wind.

Slowly, the fire died down until the nest was nothing but ashes. The baby firehawks peeped loudly, and Blaze smiled down at them. The baby firehawks took to the sky, then flew into their mothers' wings.

"Did Blaze always have that feather?" Claw asked.

The friends looked at Blaze. Among her orange and red tail feathers was a new, longer one. This feather was silver, and it glittered in the sunlight.

The firehawks gathered around Blaze, quietly peeping to one another. They seemed as surprised as Blaze was about her new feather.

Talia held her wings up to calm the crowd. "I had a vision of this feather," she said. "It signifies that Blaze will grow up to be the most powerful leader the firehawks have ever seen."

The firehawks gasped.

Tag's tummy felt funny. *If Blaze is meant to be their leader*, he thought, *then she might never return to Perodia.*

Blaze looked at her new tail feather. "I thought leaders had *golden* tail feathers," she said.

"That is true. Each firehawk leader has three golden tail feathers, and your three tail feathers will grow when you are older. But this new silver feather is very special," Talia said. "More special than the golden feathers. But it won't become magical until you are fully grown. Then you will be ready to take over as leader of the firehawks."

Tag frowned. *How long would it take for Blaze to be fully grown?* he wondered.

"Tag," Skyla whispered. "What will happen when Blaze becomes leader of the firehawks?"

Tag felt his heart sink. "We will have to leave her behind," he replied.

GOING HOME

Tag watched Blaze and the other firehawks celebrating on the beach. Blaze looked so happy. He didn't want to think about leaving her behind. The six baby firehawks flew in the air, then tumbled into the water as they learned how to fly.

"Perodia is safe since we defeated Thorn. So maybe the firehawks could come home with us?" Skyla said.

Tag looked around at the beautiful island. "They have everything they need here," he said. "This is their home. And it is Blaze's home now, too."

"I think now it is time *we* went home to Perodia," Claw said, sitting down beside them.

Tag nodded. Claw was right. They had finished their journey. They had found the firehawks. He just didn't want to say goodbye to Blaze.

"Talia," Tag said. "Are you able to open a portal back to Perodia?"

"Yes," Talia said. "As long as you still have the golden feathers and the Ember Stone."

Tag froze. He looked at his friends and saw the same realization on Blaze's and Skyla's faces.

"Where are our magical objects?" Skyla cried.

"We placed them on the stones in the Cloud Kingdom," Blaze replied. "I remember seeing them swirl around us as we fell through the portal."

"I grabbed the Ember Stone as we fell," Tag said. He pulled it out of his sack. "But I wasn't able to catch the feathers, too."

Blaze looked to her mom. "Can we open the portal with just the stone?"

Talia shook her head. "You need the golden feathers, too," she said. "Or another magical object."

"There must be a way," Claw said.

"Do you have any more golden feathers?" Tag asked Talia.

Talia shook her head. "Each firehawk leader only has three golden feathers. You found all three of mine, and they helped to bring you home. But I'm afraid I don't have any more."

"What about Blaze's new silver feather?" Skyla asked. "Could that open a portal?"

Talia thought for a moment. "Maybe," she said. "But not until it gains its magic, and that won't happen until Blaze is fully grown."

Claw frowned. "There has to be another way back to Perodia."

Tag sat on the sand. "I was hoping to become an Owl of Valor when we went home," he said. "To protect Valor Wood and Perodia."

"I know," Skyla said. Her tail drooped. "I miss home, too."

"I will help you!" Blaze said. "You helped me find my family and my home. I will help you find a way back to Perodia."

Blaze's mother shook her head. "There is no other way, Blaze," she said.

Blaze stood tall. "We have to find a way," she said. "Tag and Skyla and Claw are my friends. We will find a way back to Perodia. Together."

ABOUT THE AUTHOR

KATRINA CHARMAN has wanted to be a children's book writer ever since she was eleven, when her teacher asked her class to write an epilogue to Roald Dahl's *Matilda*. Katrina's teacher thought her writing was good enough to send to Roald Dahl himself! Sadly, she never got a reply, but this experience ignited her love of reading and writing. Katrina lives in England with her husband and three daughters. The Last Firehawk is her first early chapter book series in the U.S.

ABOUT THE ILLUSTRATOR

JUDIT TONDORA was born in Hungary and now works from her countryside studio. Her illustrations are rooted in the traditional European style but also contain elements of American mainstream style. Her characters have a vivacious retro vibe placed right into the present day: she says, "I put the good old retro together with modern style to give charisma to my illustrations."

The LAST FIREHAWK
The Golden Temple

Questions and Activities

1. **R**eread Talia's story on page 55. Why did the firehawks leave Perodia?

2. **T**alia gives gifts to Tag and Skyla. What are the gifts? How do you think they might be useful in the future?

3. **B**laze has a new feather after the hatching ceremony. What color is it? Why is this new feather important?

4. **W**hat did the friends lose when they jumped through the portal? What does this mean for their journey home?

5. **I**magine that you are exploring the Land of the Firehawks! What new sights would you find? Draw and label your own map of this new land.

Quick and Easy PAPER PLANES that *Really* Fly!

Paul Jackson

CONTENTS

INTRODUCTION

This fun book shows you how to make simple paper planes that fly brilliantly, every time. They are all quick to fold, easy to remember and can be made anywhere, any time, with ordinary paper.

Learn how to make your favorite planes well, then teach them to your friends and play games with them or have competitions - there are some ideas at the back of the book. Sharing paper planes is the best way to enjoy them.

But, a paper plane will only fly well if it is carefully made and properly thrown. So, before folding your first plane, read the next two pages to see *what* you must do, and *how* and *why*. A good paper plane is not only good fun, but also good science.

READ THIS!

Here are some important tips to help make your planes fly well.

• *Fold slowly and neatly* A plane will not fly if it is badly made. Try folding a plane twice to learn how to make it well.

• *Press every crease firmly* Sharp creases help a plane to cut through the air smoothly. Soft creases do not.

• *Fold on a table* Don't fold on your lap, in the air or on a soft surface such as a carpet.

• *Follow the drawings carefully* When folding, keep checking that your model looks like the step-by-step drawings. If it doesn't . . . don't panic! Just unfold one or two of the new creases until your model looks like an earlier drawing, then try again.

• *Read the "Throwing" instructions.* A carefully made plane will not fly well if it is thrown incorrectly. Some need to be thrown hard, others gently. Some are held and thrown in strange ways.

Adjusting the Wings

1. If your plane flies quickly upwards, stops and drops like a stone (called "stalling") . . . curl the back of the wings *gently downwards*. This will make the plane fly level.

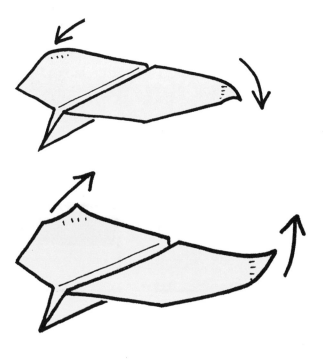

2. If your plane flies quickly downwards (called "nose diving") . . . curl the back of the wings *gently upwards*. This will make the plane fly level.

3. If your plane still doesn't fly . . . adjust the angle across the wings (called the "dihedral"). Try these dihedral shapes to see which is best for your plane:

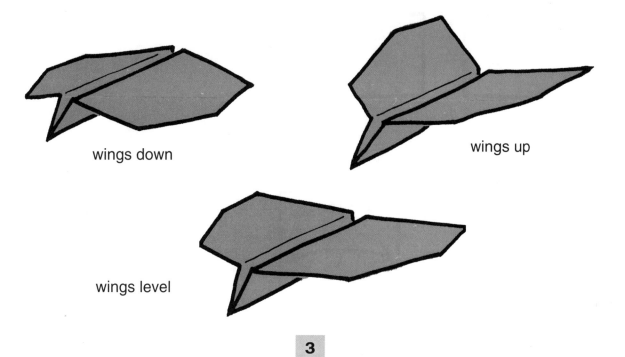

wings down

wings up

wings level

Symbols

These simple symbols explain how the planes are made. Make sure that you understand the difference between a *valley* fold and a *mountain* fold. If you confuse them, your planes will be made inside out!

valley fold

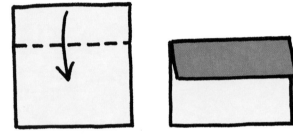

mountain fold

unfolded crease   crease, then unfold   turn the paper over

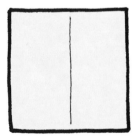 

FLOATING RING

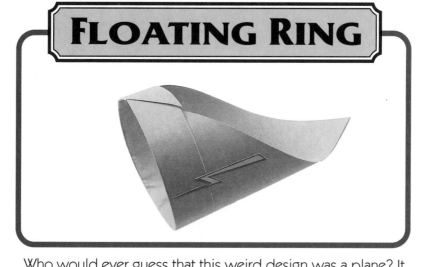

Who would ever guess that this weird design was a plane? It is only two creases, but thrown properly this amazing glider flies well. Lock the paper to make a ring at the front, then adjust it to make a neat circle. Use a square of paper, preferably thin. Airmail paper is good.

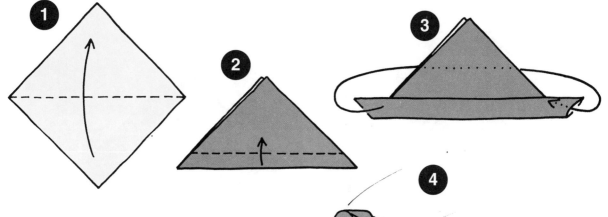

Throwing

Hold by placing your middle finger on top of the paper. Raise your arm high above your head and release gently forward with a slight flick. It will never fly if it is thrown hard or launched at the wrong angle, so practice different ways to throw it.

5

EASTERN STAR

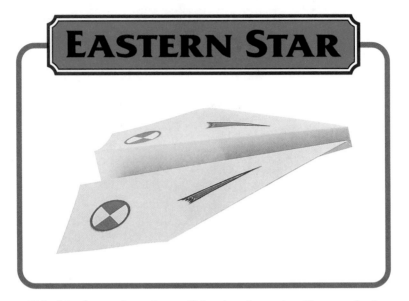

This fabulous plane from China is a true star. Thrown just right it will glide a long way, then land gently. Use European A4 paper or American 8 1/2 x 11 paper.

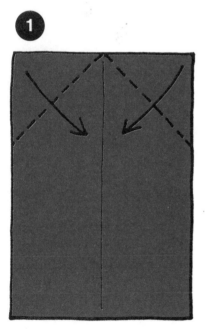

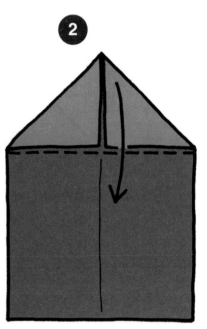

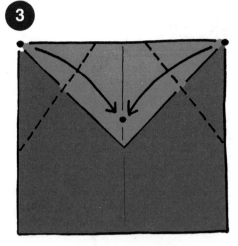

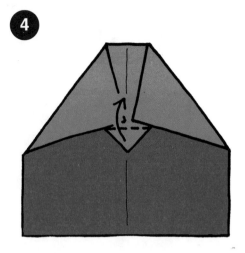

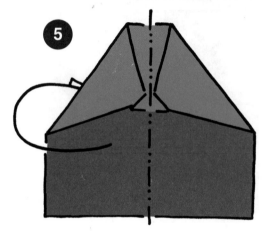

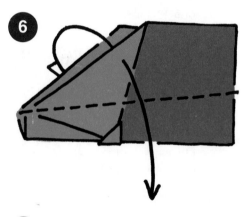

Throwing

Hold the small triangle
under the wings and
throw smoothly forward.
Don't throw it too hard.

W-WOBBLER

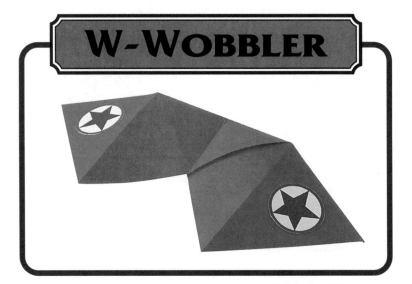

Shaped like a letter W, this strange plane is incredibly acrobatic. Look at the weird crease made in Step 1. Get it right and the rest is easy. Use the long rectangle which remains when a square is cut from European A4 paper, or use a rectangle about 8 1/2 x 4 ins (210 x 90mm).

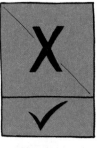

A4

or . . .

8½ins (20cms)

4ins (9cms)

1

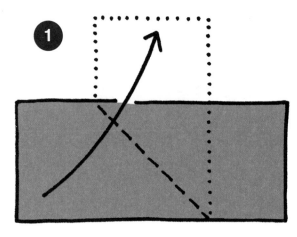

2

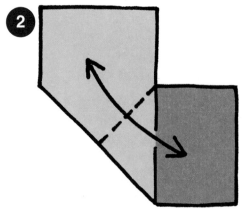

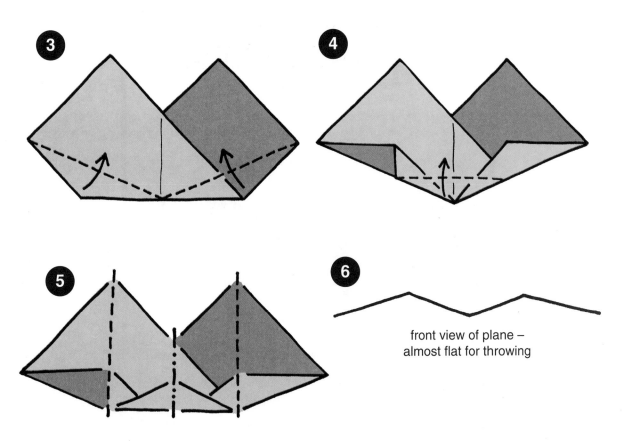

front view of plane –
almost flat for throwing

Throwing

Hold by placing your first (index) finger on top. Then bend your elbow so that your hand is above your shoulder and the plane is upside down, pointing backwards. Launch it by straightening the arm and releasing the plane gently forward. Practice the launch!

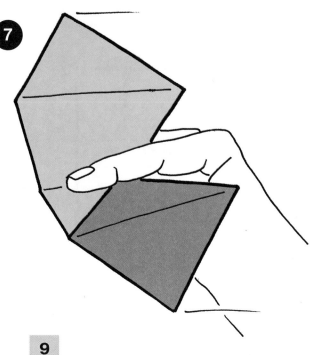

BAR FLYER

The Bar Flyer is a stable plane which flies well outdoors.
Watch how corners C&D move between Step 4 and Step 5
to make the wide bar across the nose. Use a square of paper.

1

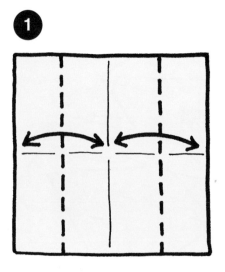

2

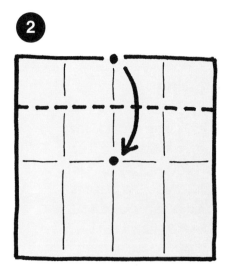

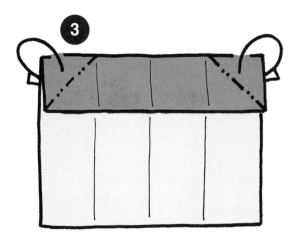

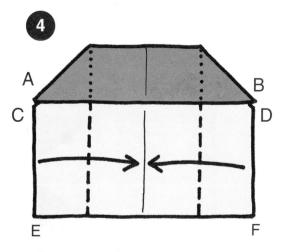

A   B
C   D
E   F

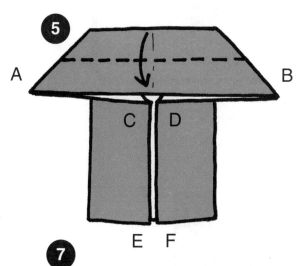

A   B
C   D
E   F

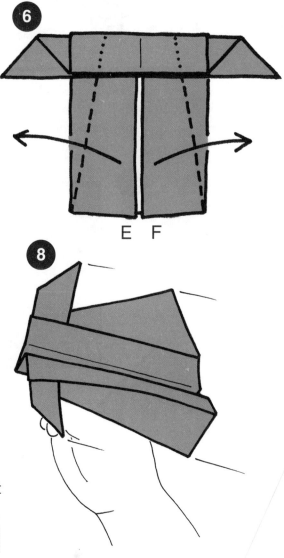

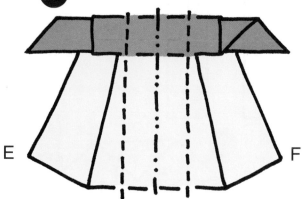

E   F

Throwing

Hold at the point of balance. Try throwing it at different speeds, sometimes high into the air.

NARROW ARROW

This terrific flyer is made from two pieces - a square and a narrow rectangle. The tail is important because it stabilizes the wings in flight. Remember to make the tail narrow, not wide.

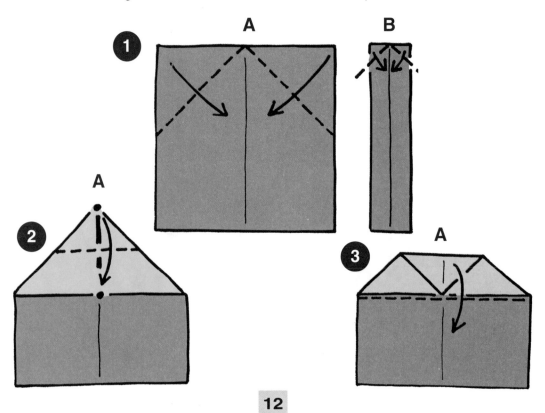

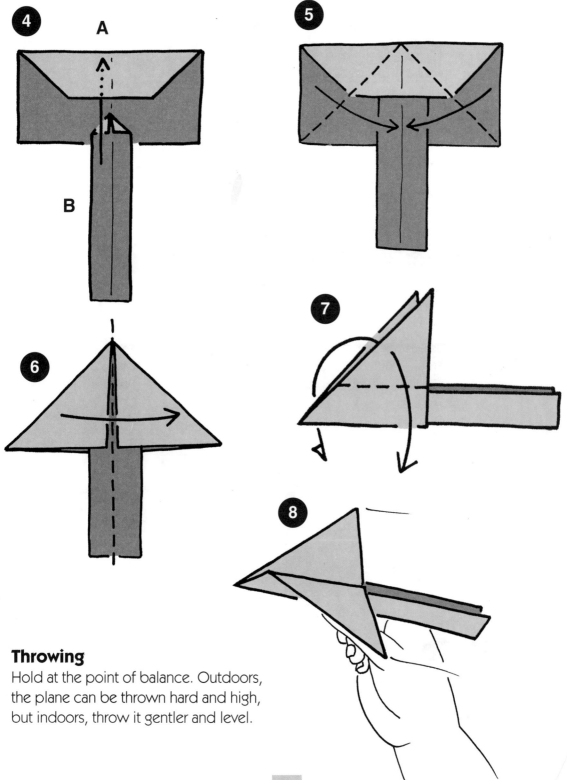

Throwing
Hold at the point of balance. Outdoors, the plane can be thrown hard and high, but indoors, throw it gentler and level.

SKY CRUISER

The small winglets at the front give this plane super stability,
so that it flies well indoors or out. Use a square of paper.

1

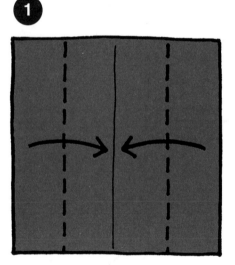

2

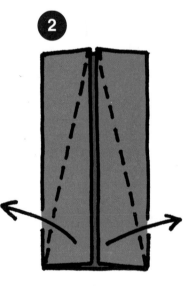

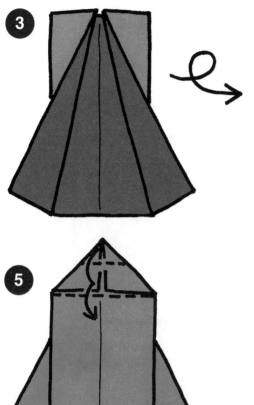

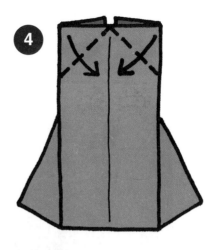

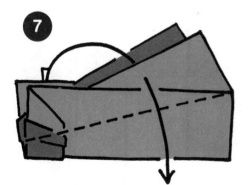

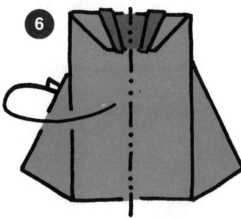

Throwing

Hold at the point of balance. Outdoors, the plane can be thrown hard and high, but indoors, throw it gentler and level.

SPACE DART

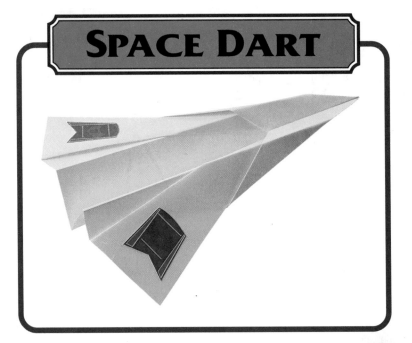

The Space Dart is perfect for target practice because its pointed nose and narrow wings mean that it flies fast and straight. Use a square of paper.

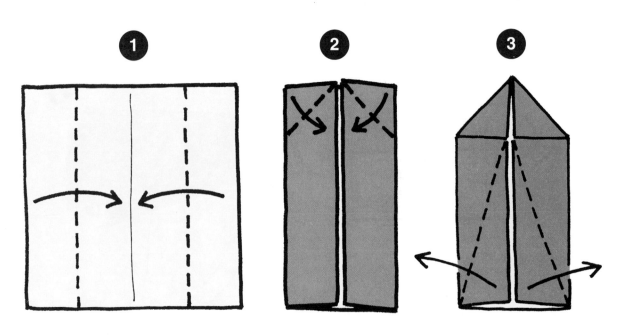

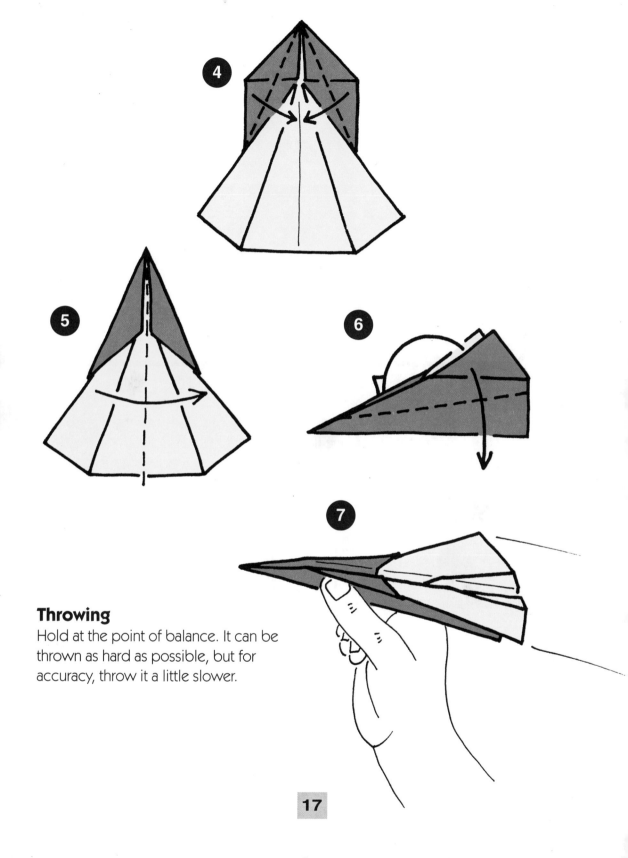

4

5

6

7

Throwing

Hold at the point of balance. It can be
thrown as hard as possible, but for
accuracy, throw it a little slower.

BOOMERANG JET

This crazy plane flies away . . . then flips over and flies back!
Thrown extra hard it sometimes keeps flying away, or performs a
loop. Notice how at Step 6, corner C is tucked deep inside the
nose to lock the plane flat. Use a square of paper.

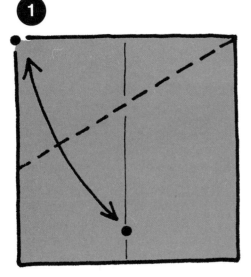

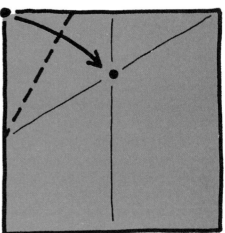

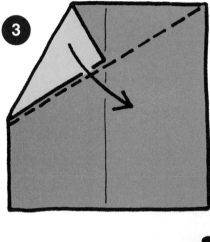

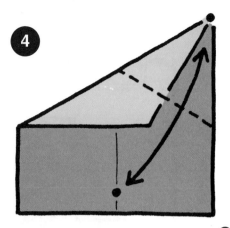

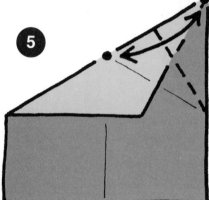

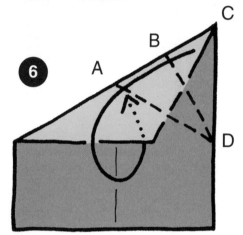

A B C D

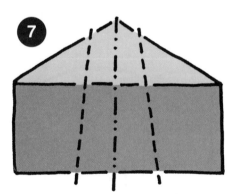

Throwing

Hold at the point of balance.
To see the boomerang effect,
throw level at a moderate speed.

FLAT FLYER

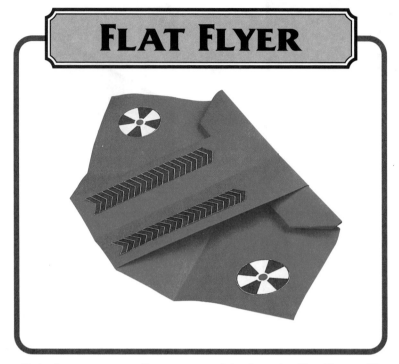

Flat planes are usually very unstable, but the Flat Flyer will fly a long way at high speed. Its strange shape means that it must be held and thrown in a strange way, so read the Throwing instructions carefully. Use European A4 paper or American 8 ½ x 11 paper, creased into quarters.

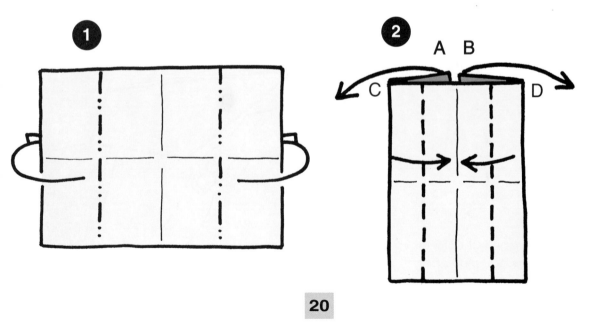

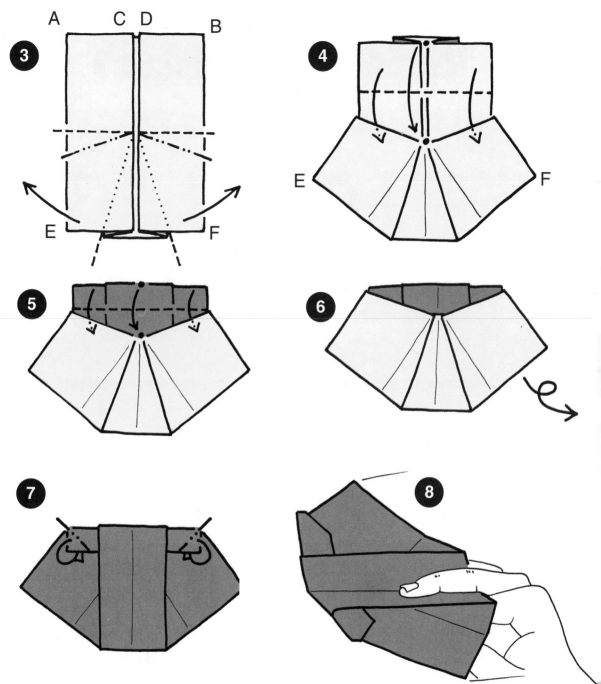

Throwing

Hold by placing your middle finger on top, and your first and third fingers underneath to support the wings. Launch by bending your elbow and flicking it firmly forward. Don't throw it high into the air.

THE ALBERT ROSS

Should this wide-winged plane be called the Albert Ross or the Albatross, the largest flying bird in the world?! Its wide wings and heavy nose mean that it flies well indoors or out. Use European A4 paper or American 8 1/2 x 11 paper.

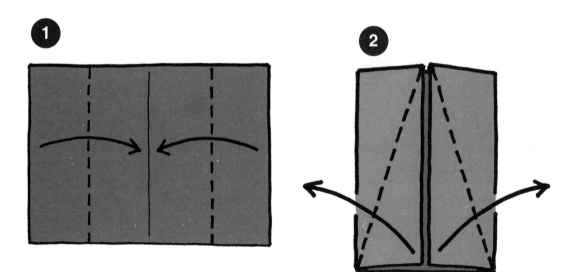

1

2

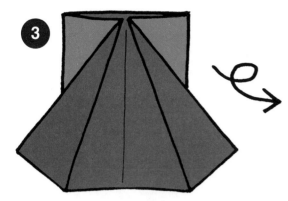

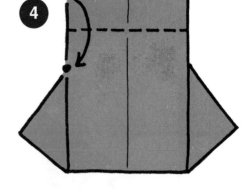

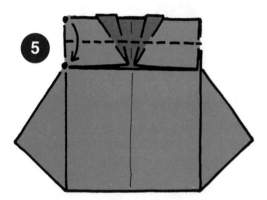

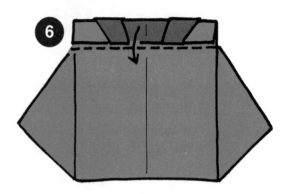

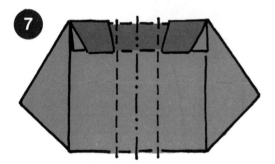

Throwing

Hold at the point of balance.
Throw with a moderate push,
either level or up into the air.

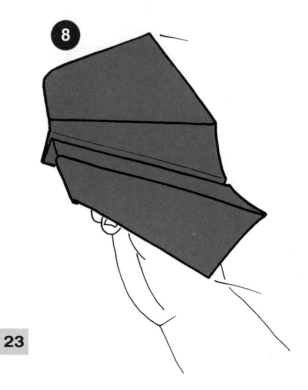

STRATO CLIMBER

Thrown high into the air, the Strato Climber will glide slowly down to earth. Notice how at Step 4, corners A&B are folded behind to look like Step 5. Use European A4 paper or American 8 ½ x 11 paper.

1

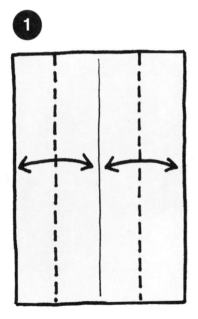

2

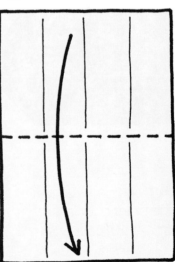

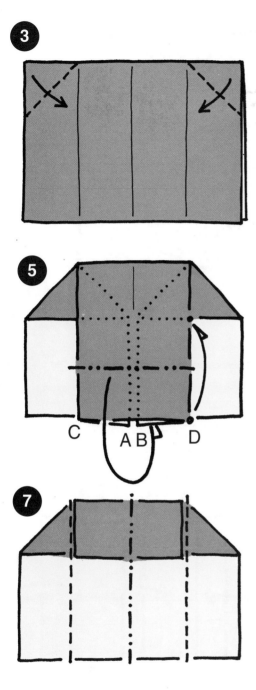

3

4

A   C   D   B

5

C   A B   D

6

7

Throwing

Hold at the point of balance.
Throw high into the air with as
much speed as possible. Also
try a gentler, level launch.

8

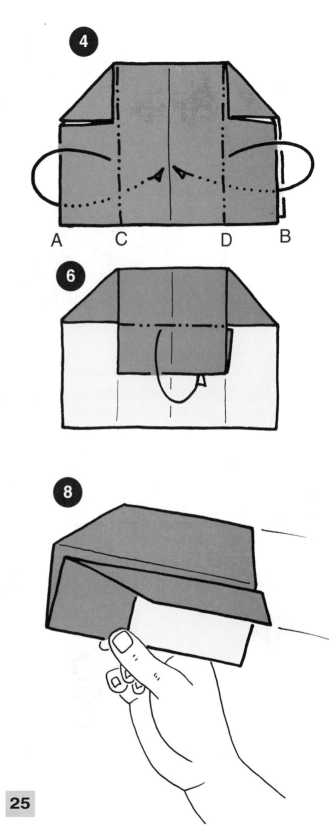

GLIDING GIRDER

This plane is bizarre! It has no crease down the center and one wing is larger than the other. But, amazingly, it flies very smoothly, sometimes in a wide circle. Be careful to throw it properly. Use a square of paper.

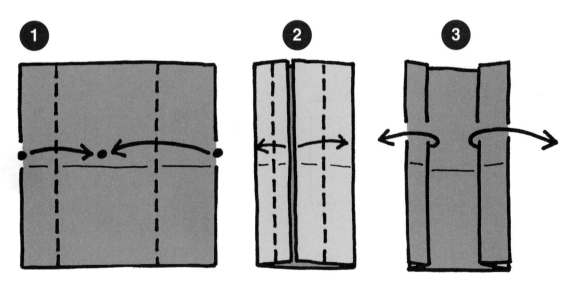

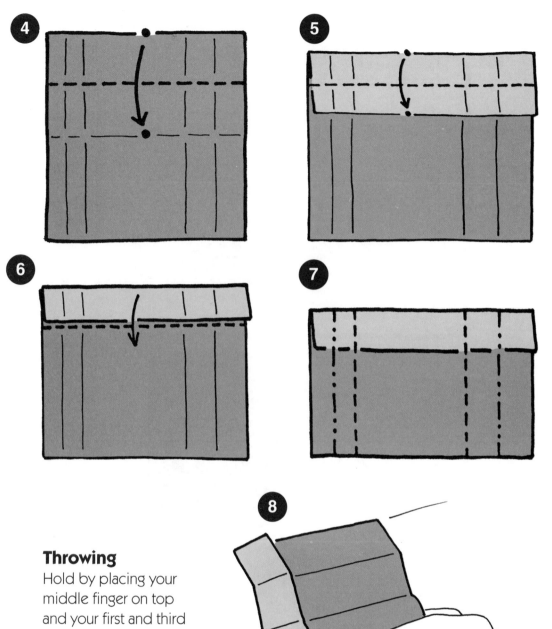

Throwing

Hold by placing your middle finger on top and your first and third fingers underneath to support the wings. Launch by flicking it smoothly and gently forwards.

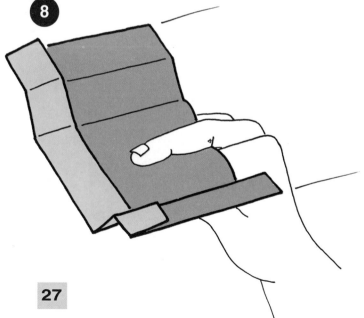

T-GLIDER

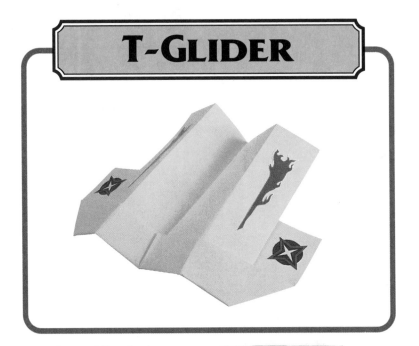

Shaped like the letter T, this very strong plane is a superb outdoor flyer. If it catches the breeze it should fly right out of sight! Use European A4 paper or American 8 ½ x 11 paper.

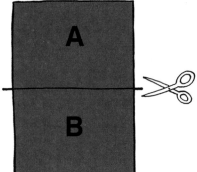

A

B

1

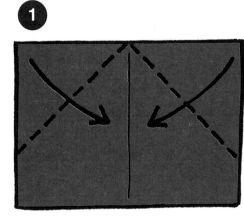

2   **A complete**

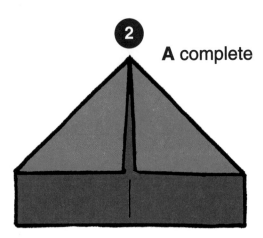

3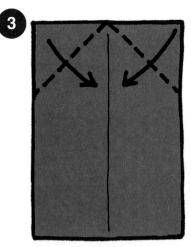

4 **B** complete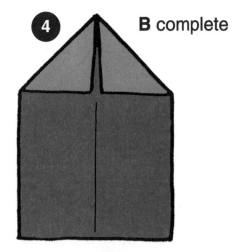

5 **A**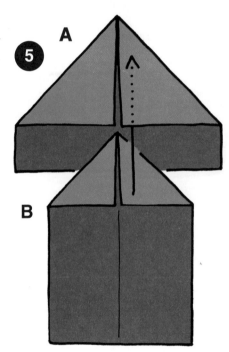

B

6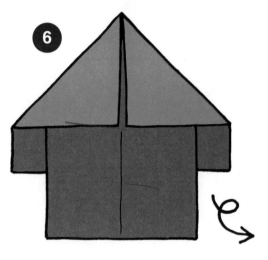

7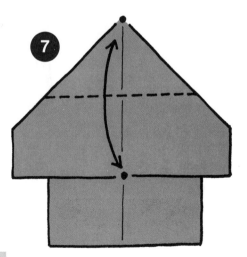

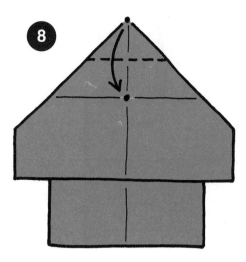

8

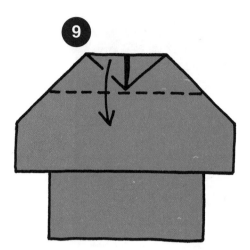

9

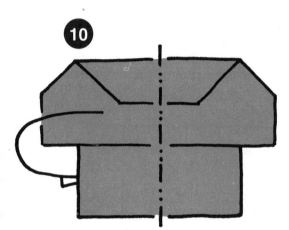

10

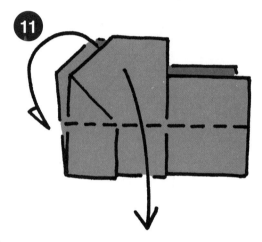

11

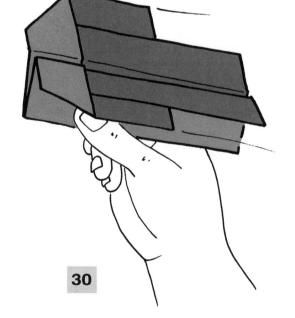

12

Throwing

Hold just forward of the point of balance. Throw it hard and high into the air . . . then be prepared to run after it as it flies away!

THINGS TO DO WITH PAPER PLANES

Distance Competition
Get together with friends and see who can throw a paper plane the furthest, or . . .

Accuracy Competition
. . . see who can throw a plane nearest to a target such as a chair or a tree, or . . .

Time Aloft Competition
. . . see who can keep a plane in the air the longest, or . . .

Golf Competition
. . . play paper plane golf! The "holes" can be things like buckets placed close together or far apart. You can include obstacles such as a narrow doorway to throw through, or a fence or an excited dog. Throw in pairs, so that each person can keep the other's score. The winner is the player who completes the course with the least number of throws.

Messages
If you want to get a message to someone nearby, but you shouldn't speak to them, write it on a plane and throw it across. Be careful to throw it accurately if you don't want someone else to read your message!

This edition published 1997 by
Flying Frog Publishing, Auburn, Maine 04210

Originally published in Great Britain in 1996 by
Michael O'Mara Books Limited, 9 Lion Yard,
Tremadoc Road, London SW4 7NQ

Quick and Easy Paper Planes that Really Fly! © copyright 1996 by Paul Jackson

The right of Paul Jackson to be identified as the author of this work has been asserted by him in accordance with the Copyright, Designs and Patents Act 1988.

ISBN 1-884628-02-8

Printed in Canada